This book is a work of fiction.
First published in 2017 by RiverFrog Limited
Kemp House
160 City Road
London
EC1V 2NX

Copyright © RiverFrog 2017
Text © Rebecca Darko and Rutendo Muzambi 2017
Illustrations © RiverFrog Limited 2017

Printed and bound in Ireland by W&G Baird

ISBN: 978-0-9956767-0-1

This book can be ordered directly from the publishers' website:
www.riverfrog.co.uk

The item should be returned or renewed by the last date stamped below.

Dylid dychwelyd neu adnewyddu'r eitem erbyn y dyddiad olaf sydd wedi'i stampio isod.

8 NOV 2023

To renew visit / Adnewyddwch ar
www.newport.gov.uk/libraries

Bella's Adventures in Africa

Riverfrog

This Book Belongs to

....

Contents

Off to Africa

Map of Africa

At last! It was the day when Bella would be leaving England to travel across Africa. Her Mum and Dad were archaeologists and they were going to Africa to examine the ruins of ancient African kingdoms. When Bella heard that she was going with them, it was a dream come true. She had always wanted to go on an adventure and she could not wait to see all the amazing African animals, especially elephants. They were her favourite animals. Bursting with excitement, Bella began to pack her suitcase and wondered what Africa would be like.

"Will you live with lions and leopards?" asked her best friend Rosie.

"I hope so," exclaimed Bella.

Bella had never been to Africa, so she was not at all sure what to expect. Eagerly, she carried on packing when Rosie suddenly leaned forward and grabbed a stuffed elephant sticking out of her suitcase.

Waving the elephant from side to side, Rosie teased, "Oh, so you're taking Cuddles with you."

Cuddles had been Bella's favourite toy for as long as she could remember. But Bella felt embarrassed. Was she too old to take Cuddles with her everywhere she went? Playfully, she snatched a pillow from underneath her duvet and tossed it at Rosie. The pillow bounced off Rosie's head and landed on the carpet. "Pillow fight!" they yelled in unison.

Before long, the girls were jumping up and down on the bed, giggling, when they heard Mum call from downstairs, "Bella. Hurry! We must leave for the airport right away."

Bella quickly shoved all her belongings into her suitcase and raced to the door.

"Promise you will visit me," she said to Rosie, hugging her tightly.

"I promise," smiled Rosie, as she waved goodbye to her friend.

The next day Bella and her parents landed in Accra, the capital city of Ghana. Throughout their flight, Bella had not stopped thinking about the animals she was going to see.

After they had landed and collected their luggage she squeezed through the crowds of people at the airport and dashed out onto the street. She looked to her left and looked to her right. But something was not quite right. There was no elephant to ride, no fearless lions chasing buffaloes, and no zebras roaming about.

"Where are all the animals?" she asked, pulling on Mum's hand.

"Oh Bella," smiled Mum. "This is the airport, not the zoo."

Disappointed, Bella watched the stream of cars coming to pick people up from the airport. She closed her eyes and hoped that they were not going to be picked up by a car.

"Maybe an elephant will come tramping along and pick us up. A great big elephant with a mighty trunk, massive floppy ears and majestic tusks," she thought to herself.

But when she opened her eyes, there was no elephant. Instead, a bright yellow taxi was parked in front of them, and Dad was busy squeezing all their bags into the taxi.

"This is not the Africa I was expecting," she muttered under her breath.

In the taxi, Dad glanced over his shoulder to the back seat and saw how miserable Bella looked. He pointed out all the beautiful things she had not looked at. She had not noticed the heat of the sun warming her skin, the colourful clothes that people wore, the palm trees that lined the streets or the beautiful beaches by the coast.

Bella realised that Ghana was very different from what she had thought. "Perhaps I have not given Ghana a chance," she said.

After a long drive through the streets of Accra they finally stopped at a big mansion.

The Mensahs

Dad told Bella that they were going to be staying with family friends, the Mensahs. Mr Mensah lived in the mansion with his daughter called Abena and their maids.

As Bella stepped out of the car, Abena ran up to her. "Akwaaba!" she exclaimed.

"Akwaa?" echoed Bella.

"Akwaaba! It means welcome," said Abena. "Welcome to Ghana!"

The maids helped them with their bags while Abena gave Bella a tour of their house. It wasn't long before the girls were laughing and giggling as if they had known each other forever.

"My Dad says there are beaches in Ghana. Can you take me to one?" asked Bella.

"Of course, let's go to the beach tomorrow," suggested Abena, happily. Abena could not wait to show Bella around. "There are horses, crabs and even sea turtles. You will love it."

That night when they went to bed, they were both excited about their trip to the beach. Suddenly Bella did not feel so bad. She looked forward to seeing what the next day in Ghana would be like.

A trip to the Beach

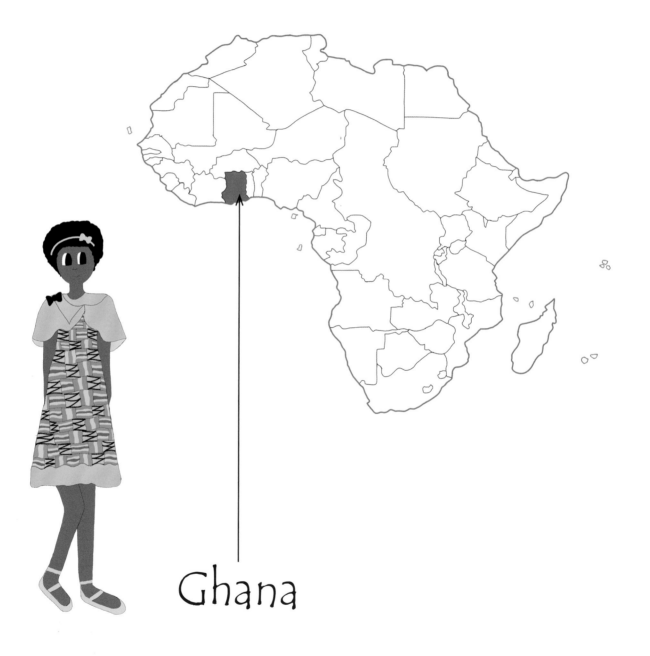

Ghana

Bella was overjoyed to be going on an adventure in Ghana with her new friend, Abena. Luckily it was a sunny day and so Bella could not wait to get to the beach. She had woken up early, packed her bag and was ready to go. Now, all she had to do was wait for Abena, whose afro was being neatly combed by one of the maids. Just when she thought the maid had finished, Abena began to try on some of her many sun hats.

"Not this one, not that one, and definitely not this one," said Abena.

Bella could not wait any longer. "Its time to go," she said. "We can't waste anymore time."

Bella grabbed her bag and the girls rushed to the door.

However, standing directly in front of them blocking their way was Abena's father, Mr Mensah. He stared at the girls in amazement and asked, "Where are you going?"

"To the beach," replied Bella.

Mr Mensah was amused that the girls thought they could go to the beach alone.

"No, not today," said Mr Mensah, shaking his head. "You are both coming to the cocoa farm with me."

"Oh, not the cocoa farm again," Abena whispered in Bella's ear.

"How boring!" replied Bella.

"Please Papa!" she pleaded, looking into her father's eyes. Her father always found it difficult to refuse anything his daughter asked but this was the one thing he never allowed. "How can I have any fun if you never let me have any adventures on my own?"

"No, I can't let you go out on your own," he said sternly. "I need to make sure you are safe."

Abena hated the way her father treated her like a little child.

After much grumbling, they followed him, dragging their feet and sat in the cool shade of a cocoa tree. Mr Mensah owned several cocoa farms and so he had a lot of business to attend to.

The girls had been waiting for what seemed like forever, when suddenly Bella blurted out, "It's not fair! Why should we have to sit here when we could be out having fun at the beach."

Bella never liked sitting around for too long and was eager to explore. After all, this was her second day in Ghana and she had not yet done anything fun and there was no way she was going to spend the rest of the day sitting under a cocoa tree. She just had to hatch a plan.

Abena, on the other hand, was used to waiting for her father all the time. She was quite glad to have someone to keep her company instead of just playing games on her mobile phone.

Just then, Mr Mensah called out, "Time to go girls. I have some more work to do at the market." At last they were finally leaving the cocoa farm.

As Mr Mensah drove down the bumpy roads, past the children playing jump rope, he was caught up in a traffic jam. Bella was staring out of the window when she heard a loud voice behind her, "Accra, Accra, Accra!"

It was a bus conductor who was hanging at the edge of a moving bus calling for passengers. To her left side there was another sound. A woman, carefully balancing a basket of food on her head, was gently tapping at the car window, offering food for sale.

Abena bought frozen yogurt and plantain crisps for herself and Bella. As they ate, Bella began to share her plan with Abena.

"There is only one way we will get to the beach today," she whispered, "when we get to the market we should sneak away."

Abena paused. She had never ran away from her father before and she knew he would be furious.

"Maybe it's not a good idea," she thought.

But Abena was also eager to have a fun adventure.

When they finally reached the market, it was buzzing with activity. Bella was amazed by how colourful everything was.

"Fresh fish over here!" shouted a woman standing behind a market stall. "Come and get some fresh fish."

The market sellers sold lots of different items. They had tomatoes, bundles of yam, jars of jam and even red juicy lobsters. Fascinated, they continued walking around the market until they reached the shop where Mr Mensah planned to sell his bags of bean pods.

As the shopkeeper weighed and checked the bags, Mr Mensah turned to the girls and commanded, "Wait here."

However, as soon as his back was turned, Bella grabbed Abena's hand and whispered, "Quick! Let's sneak off now."

The girls ran as fast as they could until they found a bus going to the beach.

Abena had never been on a bus before. She was surprised to find it packed full of people.

 "We really should've called a taxi," she complained.

The girls squeezed in between a large man and a woman holding a baby.

Abena felt uncomfortable but fortunately, the bus conductor announced, "Next stop is the beach."

When they arrived, they saw the blue sea and heard the sound of the waves gently splashing against the rocks. Glancing up and down the beach Bella found the perfect spot to sit and spread her towel.

She was about to unpack her bag when Abena shouted, "Race you into the sea."

Full of excitement, Abena threw her phone onto the towel and sprinted across the beach. Bella rushed to catch up with her friend.

The girls kneeled down at the water's edge to catch their breath with the scent of the salty air filling their noses. "Let's write our names on the sand," suggested Bella. Carefully, they carved their names into the sand with their fingers and watched as the water came in and washed away their writing. They looked around, wondering what to do next. Then, behind the beach chairs and past the row of palm trees, Bella spotted two horses.

Bella ran up to the horses, startling them.

"You've got to be gentle," whispered Abena, "you frightened the poor thing."

"I didn't mean to scare it," said Bella, who then gently stroked the horse's neck.

The horse whinnied happily. With the owner's permission, Bella and Abena each climbed onto a horse's back and the horses trotted across the soft sand.

They were having so much fun when a sudden flash of lightning lit up the sky. The once blue sky had suddenly turned grey and the girls could feel heavy drops of rain splattering on their shoulders.

"Jump off!" warned the owner of the horses. "It looks as though a huge storm is on its way."

At that moment, there was a loud clap of thunder. The girls slid off the horse and watched as the owner led the horses to their stable.

"I want to go home now," cried Abena.

The two girls hurried back to the spot where they had left their belongings only to find an empty bag. Bella tipped the bag upside down, shook it from side to side and pulled out all the pockets but the bag was empty.

"Oh no!" shrieked Bella. "Somebody has stolen all our stuff!"

"Oh how could you have left your bag here Bella," cried Abena.

Bella felt bad. "Well I can be a little clumsy with my stuff. My parents are always telling me to look after my things properly," she admitted.

Abena was used to her maids always looking after her things. She could hardly believe what was happening. Exhausted and wet, they huddled together under a coconut tree and looked on as people ran from the beach.

What were they going to do? All their money had been in Bella's bag so they could not get on a bus and Abena's father had probably left the market by now.

"If only I had listened to my father," thought Abena.

Her eyes started to fill up with tears. Bella saw this and hugged her.

A while later, the dark clouds began to disappear. Slowly, the sun started to rise and the wind simmered down. In the distance, the girls could see a figure walking up the beach, waving at them.

Nervously, they stared as the figure drew closer and closer. Then Abena recognised the orange jacket and the red and green umbrella. She leapt up and rushed towards the figure.

"Papa! Papa! Papa!" she screamed, throwing her arms around her father and hugging him tightly.

"Abena! Thank goodness you are here," said Mr Mensah. "I was so worried."

"I should never have gone to the beach," she sobbed, "you were right."

Mr Mensah looked at her and smiled. "No, you were right. How can you ever have any fun if I don't let you have on your own adventures? If I had listened to you, I would have warned you about the terrible storm."

The girls promised to never sneak away to the beach again and Mr Mensah took them back home. By the time they reached home, Mum and Dad had already returned. They had been working at the ruins of the Ashanti Kingdom and wanted to tell Bella all about the great Kings of Ghana. However they had been told the girls were missing and were worried.

As soon as the girls entered the house, Mum rushed to the door. With a sigh of relief, she wrapped them each in a thick warm blanket while Dad handed the girls a hot cup of cocoa.

Bella felt awful. She loved exploring so much that sometimes she would do anything for an adventure. Mum and Dad were so disappointed in her behaviour that they told Bella that she would not receive any pocket money for the rest time they were in Ghana.

"Dinner is ready," said one of the maids, placing a big portion of banku, okra stew and jollof rice on the table.

As they ate, Abena was puzzled by something.

"But Papa," she said, "why are you not as angry with me as I expected?"

Mr Mensah turned to Abena and explained that after her mother passed away he was terrified of losing her too so he had become so overprotective that he had forgotten that she needed to have fun too. From that day on, Mr Mensah listened to his daughter more and Abena never sneaked away again.

The Safari

South Africa

Bella longed to go on a Safari, so when she arrived in South Africa she was keen to go on a safari adventure. She could not wait to see all the wild animals she had read about ever since she was little. However, by the time they reached the game lodge where they were going to be staying she was already fast asleep.

When morning came, Bella was awoken by the sounds of hippos noisily grunting to each other and the laughter of hyenas from afar. Full of excitement, she listened closely and could hear thumping noises approaching the lodge. Then the noise grew louder and louder. Bella knew just what it was and leaped out of bed.

"Elephants!" she screamed, sticking her head out of the window, hoping to catch sight of them. However, when she looked around the elephants were out of sight. Instead, she saw a boy and a girl sitting on a bench opposite her window.

"I wonder if they know where the elephants have gone to," she thought.

The pair smiled at Bella and beckoned at her to join them.

They were two friends, a girl called Thandiwe and a boy called Johan, whose fathers worked as game rangers at the lodge. When Bella asked them about the elephants she could hear from her room, they led her to a waterhole nearby.

"Every morning many animals come here to drink," said Johan, as they all sat in a hide overlooking the waterhole.

"Here come the buffalos!" said Thandiwe.

Johan jumped up and copied the buffalos: "Slurp, slurp, slurp," he smiled.

Bella laughed.

Next came the hippos for their turn, and Johan bent down to mimic the hippos, "glug, glug, glug," he said, grinning like the hippo.

One of the large hippos gave him a stern look and opened its mouth wide, revealing its huge tusks. Startled, Johan lost his footing and landed straight in a puddle, which sent the girls into a fit of giggles.

"Silly hippo," he said, laughing along with the girls. At the other end of the waterhole, past the lions who quietly gazed at a couple of zebras, Bella spotted a herd of elephants.

"There are the elephants!" she said, pointing with a big grin.

Among the herd was a mother elephant and her baby. She watched as the calf filled his long trunk with water and sprayed it everywhere. He rolled around, playing by the waterhole. He was having so much fun that he did not notice his mother leave with the rest of the herd.

In his hurry to catch up with his mother, the calf didn't look where he was going and fell into a well. His mother tried to pull him out with her trunk but she just couldn't manage to get him out. She had no choice but to leave with the rest of the herd.

"Oh no!" shouted Bella. "We've got to help him."

She was about to run towards the calf when Thandiwe warned, "We can't go to the elephants on our own. It's dangerous."

Wasting no time, Johan rushed to the lodge, "Father! Father! Come quickly," he called.

The rangers knew just what to do and rescued him from the well. As soon as he was out, he tried to run and search for his mother but he stumbled. He had hurt his leg during the fall.

"We must take care of him until we find his mother!" exclaimed Bella.

"That's a good idea, but first we need to call the vet to come and treat him," replied the rangers.

The vet was called and she treated the calf's leg.

"Now that Ingane's better, is everybody ready for an adventure?" asked one of the rangers. "Do you want to go to the beach or on a safari?"

Johan and Thandiwe were keen to go to the beach but Bella had never seen wild animals before, so they all agreed to go to on a Safari drive.

"But what about Ingane?" asked Bella. "Isn't he going to be lonely?"

At that moment, she heard familiar voices behind her. It was Mum and Dad, who had just come back from an archaeological site, the ruins of the Mapungubwe Kingdom. They had been examining ancient artefacts found in the palaces of the wealthy Kingdom.

"Oh, what happened to this poor baby elephant?" asked Mum, looking at Ingane.

When Bella told them what had happened Mum offered to stay and keep Ingane company while everyone else went for the drive, as she loved elephants just as much as Bella. Dad was eager to join the safari and grabbed a basket of food.

"Maybe we can look for Ingane's mother on the way," suggested the rangers.

As they drove along the bumpy roads the rangers showed them the animals in the game park.

"If you look to your right, you will see a crash of rhinos, and to your left there are a couple of buffalos," announced the rangers. Bella wanted to know everything about the animals they could see around them and she listened attentively to the rangers.

However, Johan's attention was elsewhere. He had spotted a troop of obnoxious baboons that were sat nearby. He caught the attention of one that was particularly grumpy. Daringly, he stuck his tongue out at it.

When Thandiwe saw what he was up to she whispered, "We will be in trouble if they think we have been bothering the baboons."

But Johan did not listen and carried on teasing them. This angered the baboons.

The troop loped towards the truck and one of them tried to snatch his leather sling bag. Johan shivered but he held on tightly. Together all the children clung onto each other, until Johan pulled his bag away from it.

"Well done Johan," whispered Bella.

However, what they had not realised was that after a few moments, two of the baboons had come back and had jumped onto the roof of the truck.

While this was going on they were all distracted by Dad, who was busy fiddling with his new camera and taking pictures of anything that moved.

"Antelopes," he shouted excitedly, flashing his camera. "Warthogs," he continued snapping several more pictures. "What's that over there?" asked Dad, pointing at something far away.

"Perhaps it's Ingane's mother," said Bella.

There, past the clump of trees, was an animal nibbling on acacia tree leaves. As they drove closer they could see the creature curling its purple tongue around the sharp thorns of the tree to get to the leaves.

"No, it's not Ingane's mother," said Bella quietly, so as to not frighten the animal. "It's a giraffe."

Beaming from ear to ear with excitement, she begged the rangers to stop. The rangers switched off the engine to avoid scaring the giraffe. In an instant, Bella reached for a couple of carrots and climbed out of the truck.

She gazed up into its big bright eyes and the graceful giraffe lowered its neck.

Seeing this, Johan leaped out of the truck and yelled, "That looks like fun, I'm coming to join you!"

"Me too," yelled Thandiwe.

But, just as they got close, the giraffe stretched its neck and spotted the naughty baboons on top of the safari truck. At once, it quickly galloped off into the distance.

They were all walking back to the truck when they stepped into something sticky and smelly. "Eww!" screamed Bella. "What is this?"

Johan laughed, "It's elephant dung."

The rangers could see that the dung was fresh.

"This must mean the herd of elephants is nearby," they said.

"And Ingane's mother!" exclaimed Bella.

As they cleaned the dung from their shoes, Bella could feel her tummy rumbling. She walked to the back of the truck to get out a basket of food when she was startled by three shadows.

"Oh no," yelled Bella. "They're back again."

There, in front of her, were two cheeky baboons rummaging through the basket of food that Mum had prepared for them. A couple more baboons climbed down from the roof of the truck and began munching on their food. Within minutes they had scattered the contents of the basket everywhere. One of the hungry baboons took a big bite of the sandwich and chucked it on the ground, while another ate all the fruit.

"That one is drinking from your water bottle," said Thandiwe to Bella.

The rangers got out of the truck to pick up some of the food. But before they could do so, the baboons snatched up all the food and dashed into the forest.

"Oh no, they have eaten everything," sighed Bella.

"Don't worry, I've got some biltong in my pocket," said Thandiwe, sharing her snack with everyone. But the snack did not fill them up for long and the rangers decided it was time for them to go back home.

They were all exhausted and hungry. On the way back, Bella stared out of the truck and wondered whether the herd of elephants had gone back to the water hole.

Eventually, they got back to the lodge. When they arrived, the smell of smoky sausages greeted them. Bella's mouth began to water. To their delight Mum had prepared a barbecue of sausages, lamb chops and ostrich steak.

"A braai. Now this looks delicious," said one of the rangers as he went to put more sausages on the grill.

Johan and Thandiwe went to the table to get some plates. While Mum and the rangers served the food, Bella walked to Ingane, who was grazing on the grass behind them. Feeling playful, he dipped his trunk into a bucket of water and sprayed her.

"Water fight!" shouted Johan, carrying a bucket of water.

Thandiwe ran to join in and before long they were all splashing water at each other. Ingane was having fun but every now and then, he would turn and stare at the waterhole. Bella wished he could stay with them forever, but she knew he was missing his mother.

Just then, they heard Mum calling, "Come and finish your food, then you can play later."

As Bella helped herself to a plate of food, she spotted a herd of elephants in the distance. There, at the very back of the herd, behind the other elephants, stood Ingane's mother, searching for her baby.

"Look!" screamed Bella, pointing at the waterhole.

"His mother has come back for him," she jumped.

In unison, Thandiwe and Johan exclaimed, "We must get him at once!"

Without a moment to lose, the rangers led Ingane to the waterhole. As soon as he saw his mother, he flapped his ears excitedly and ran to her as fast as he could. Jubilant, his mother wrapped her trunk around her baby and two loud trumpets of joy were heard.

"Hooray!" they all shouted out loud.

"Well done for helping to find Ingane's mother!" exclaimed the rangers. "As a treat we will take you to the beach."

At once, they got ready and made their way to the beach.

To Bella's amazement, this was no ordinary beach. There were penguins waddling on the beach. "Penguins? In Africa?" asked Bella.

Thandiwe and Johan laughed, "This must be your first time in South Africa. There are penguins here too."

They took off their shoes and raced into the water.

"I will have to write to my best friend Rosie who lives in England, to tell her all about South Africa's penguins and our amazing adventure with Ingane," smiled Bella.

The Festival of Masks

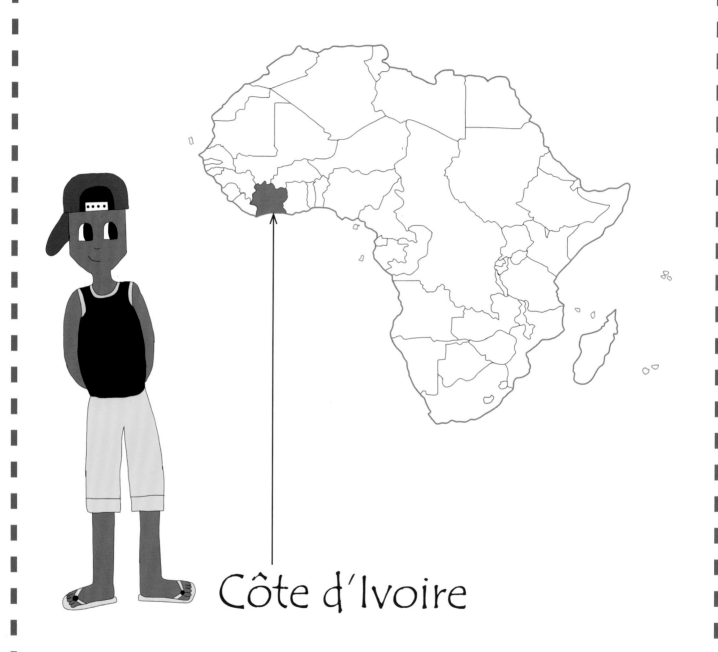

Côte d'Ivoire

This week Bella and her parents were in Côte d'Ivoire. Bella had hoped to make new friends but she could not speak a word of French. As they strolled around the city, past the high-rise buildings, all she heard was people speaking in French.

"Bonjour madam," they said. "Bonjour, Bonjour!" they replied.

It was too much to bear.

"There must be a way I can understand," she thought. "Maybe I should use my dictionary?"

She pulled out a small dictionary from her backpack and quickly flipped through the pages, trying to learn French as she walked along. But it was impossible to concentrate with the sounds of passing cars roaring in her ears.

"This is hopeless," she muttered.

How was she possibly meant to enjoy the festival of masks the next day if she could not understand the language?

Frustrated, Bella was packing her dictionary away when she saw a boy sitting beside a stall, happily whistling away.

"Hello," called the boy, whose name was Pierre. "Would you like to buy a bag of cashew nuts?"

Amazed, Bella exclaimed, "Mum he speaks English!"

"Of course I do!" Pierre replied, "I also speak French and Dioula."

Pierre offered to teach Bella French and before long, he was telling Bella all about Côte d'Ivoire. He had lived there his whole life and knew great places to visit. Pierre explained that the Festival of Masks was the people's way of paying respect to the spirit of the forest.

"It brings people together," he said proudly.

Just then, Mum and Dad interrupted him, announcing that it was time for them to go. They had a very important archaeological project to do at the museum.

"Can't I stay for a little bit longer?" pleaded Bella.

Mum and Dad could see that Bella and Pierre were getting along so well that they agreed for her to stay at the stall since the museum was opposite Pierre's stall. Pierre taught Bella French as he waited for more customers. It wasn't long before a tall boy hobbled towards them on crutches. "I haven't eaten all day," said the boy, staring at Pierre and begging for a bag of cashew nuts. Pierre was a kind-hearted boy, who always saw the good in everyone but he was also gullible. Pierre felt sorry for the boy.

"Yes, here is a bag for free," he smiled.

However, as the boy was walking away, he threw the crutches down and let out a loud laugh at how he had tricked Pierre out of his cashew nuts. When Bella saw this, she realised the boy had been dishonest and warned Pierre to be wary.

Just then, an odd-looking man with big hair, that was starting to go grey, walked up to them. He wore dark blue boots with soles that flapped as he walked. They were covered in dirt. Walking beside him was a little boy who looked just as scruffy.

"May we have ten bags of nuts?" asked the man.

Happily, Pierre placed the bags of nuts into a carrier bag.

"Run along now, I will meet you back home," said the man, giving the bags to the little boy.

Bella and Pierre waited for the man to pay and stared as he anxiously searched his pockets over and over again. He pulled out the inside of his pockets and sighed, "I cannot find my wallet."

"Oh, no!" cried Bella.

"Unfortunately my money is in my wallet which I must have left at home," said the man.

Pierre thought for a second. He turned to Bella who was looking at the man's scruffy boots and ragged clothes.

"He can't possibly have enough money," she whispered, shaking her head.

"Just promise you will come back later and pay me," said Pierre, feeling hopeful.

The man looked at Pierre gratefully. He promised and went on his way. They waited and waited, but the man never came back. Just then, Bella saw a someone coming towards them.

"I think the man is coming back," she said.

But Pierre hushed her. He knew exactly who it was.

He jumped from his stool and crouched under the bridge.

"Quick! Come here," he whispered. "I don't want them to see me."

"But why?" asked Bella, joining him.

Pierre explained it was a group of bullies from his school. His mother was poor and could barely afford to send him to school. So while the other students at his school were having fun during their school holidays, Pierre had decided to help his mother to pay for his school fees by selling nuts.

"If they see me, they will laugh at me," he sighed.

But one of the bullies spotted his green cap sticking out from under the bridge.

"Ha ha, it's Pierre selling on the roadside again," teased a girl. This made the other bully chuckle loudly.

"And look, he has got his girlfriend with him today," said another bully, pointing at Bella.

Pierre was embarrassed but he was determined to help his mother. He would never sell any nuts if he continued hiding away under the bridge. Feeling brave, he crawled out from under bridge.

"I don't care if you laugh at me," said Pierre, sternly. "I am not scared of bullies anymore."

Surprised, the bullies looked at each other. Pierre had never stood up to them before and they didn't know what to do. Bella stood beside Pierre and confronted the bullies too.

"What is so wrong with selling nuts anyway?" she said.

The trio did not have an answer. Instead, they ran off. It was now almost sunset and Pierre had not made any money that day.

"How will I pay for my school fees now?" he sighed.

Bella thought for a moment. After she had helped Pierre to close his stall, she said, "If you come with me and my parents to the festival of masks tomorrow," she suggested, "you will surely get a lot of customers."

And they agreed to try this out. The next day Pierre met Bella at the bridge again and they set off for the festival. On their way Pierre decided to pass by different shops to try and sell his nuts. Most of the shop owners were too busy to stop for him. But as he was about to give up a tailor spotted him and called him into her shop. She liked cashew nuts and wanted to buy six bags. Pierre handed her the bags, and then Bella noticed two beautiful outfits that they could wear to the festival and urged Pierre to try them on.

Feeling handsome in his green outfit, Pierre announced, "I'm the prince of Côte d'Ivoire." He imagined them sitting on a throne, in their very own palace and turned to Bella, "Where is my princess?"

Giggling, Bella replied, "Your princess? I don't know where your princess is. I am a Queen."

"Then I will be your king," laughed Pierre.

They carried on joking until they heard Mum calling. It was nearly time for the festival to begin. Running out of the shop in a hurry, they forgot to collect the money from the tailor for the nuts.

Moments later, they arrived at the festival. There were hundreds of cheerful people lining the streets watching the performers who wore elaborate masks and vibrant outfits.

It was not long before Pierre found the perfect spot to sell and soon after people flocked round him to buy his cashew nuts. Pierre was overjoyed. By now, the festival was in full swing. The dancers swayed their hips from side to side, to the beat of the drums.

The rhythm of the pounding drum got Mum excited.

"We have to dance," said Mum, grabbing Dad's hand.

The drummers continued pounding their drums whilst Mum and Dad swayed and twirled.

"Come and join us Bella," yelled Dad, as he started doing his robot dance.

"This so embarrassing," Bella told Pierre, covering her face with her hands.

Luckily, the crowd was friendly. They clapped and cheered loudly for Mum and Dad. Soon after, Pierre persuaded Bella to join in too. They sang and danced along with everyone for the rest of the day. Bella had never had so much fun before. She realised that she did not need to speak French to enjoy herself in Côte d'Ivoire after all.

After the festival, Pierre counted the money he had made. He was disappointed. He had not made enough money. It was then that he finally remembered that they had forgotten to take the money from the tailor. That night, as Bella draped her mosquito net over her bed, getting ready to sleep, she thought of Pierre. She wondered how Pierre was ever going to get enough money to pay for school.

Early the next morning, Bella went back to help Pierre at the stall. As they were setting up the stall the tailor they had met the previous day approached them.

"I have come to give you the money you forgot to take," she said, "and I have also got something special for you."

The kind tailor reached into her bag and pulled out the bright green outfit from the day before. Pierre was so happy, "Oh thank you! I guess I really can be the Prince of Côte d'Ivoire," he grinned, proud of his new outfit.

Just as she was leaving, someone else came to the stall. It was the odd-looking man who had not paid for the nuts the day before but this time, he was smartly dressed.

"Oh no," thought Bella, "He must be after some more free nuts."

The man turned to Pierre and said in a deep, calm voice, "I am the new headmaster of your school." He explained that the boy with him the day before had recognised Pierre and told him that Pierre also attended his school.

"You are a generous and good-hearted boy," he smiled, "and so I have decided to do something for you in return."

Bella was puzzled.

"But you can't possibly be the headmaster," she interrupted, "yesterday your clothes were dirty and your hair is so wild."

"I was in the garden working just before I met you and that is why my clothes were dirty and scruffy. As for my hair, I love it just the way it is," replied the headmaster.

He reached into his bag and handed Pierre the money he had promised him. Then he also offered to pay Pierre's school fees. Pierre's face lit up. He was so happy he could not stop smiling. "Merci! Merci!" he said.

"As for you, young lady, I hope you learnt an important lesson," said the headmaster, turning to Bella. "You should never judge a person by how they look."

Bella felt silly. Despite this, she was glad for Pierre. Everything was going to be alright after all.

A Surprise Visit

Zimbabwe

Bella had been staying with her grandmother, Gogo, who lived in the suburbs of Zimbabwe. Gogo was a fun, laid-back grandmother but there was just one problem. Bella had no-one else to hang around with. She sat on a swing under a purple flowering jacaranda tree, wishing she could play with her cousins but they lived in a village many miles away. As for her parents, they were working in another town, at the Great Zimbabwe ruins, a famous ancient Kingdom from many years ago.

Bella wondered whether she was ever going to have an adventure in Zimbabwe. But she had not realised that Gogo was planning a surprise for her.

"Bella, get ready," called Gogo. "We must to go to the airport now. I have a special visitor I want you to meet."

Bella wondered who the visitor could be. Just as they entered the airport, they saw a couple of people running away from something, shouting, "Katsi, katsi."

Bella was puzzled. But she followed the sound and soon spotted a small ginger cat bothering people. The cat had knocked over a basket of fruit from a woman's hand. It flew into the air and landed on a man carrying several bags. One after the other, the bags fell to the floor and soon, there was a pile.

In front of the man, was a girl with long blonde hair running after the cat.

"Mittens, Mittens. Where are you?" the girl called out.

Her voice was strangely familiar.

Bella gasped in surprise. It was her best friend Rosie, who had travelled from England to be with her.

Bella ran up to her to give her a big hug, but before she could Mittens jumped into her arms.

"Miaow, Miaow," he purred loudly. Mittens was a playful cat who loved exploring his surroundings and was always getting into mischief. He had caused a lot of trouble at the airport and people were not happy with him.

"What a mess!" a woman called out. "Who is responsible for this?" asked another.

Gogo knew it was time to go. She took the girls to a small restaurant at the airport to escape the chaos Mittens had caused. "We better let you nap in here before you cause any more trouble," said Gogo as she placed Mittens in his pink stroller.

At the restaurant, Gogo ordered food for herself and the girls. When the waiter came to give them their food, he asked, "Would you like anything for your baby?" He kneeled down to the stroller to get a closer look, when he suddenly jumped back. "Aargh. Katsi!" he gasped.

"Don't be afraid," said Bella. She did not know that the waiter believed that cats were bad luck. In fact, he did not like to be around cats for too long. Unfortunately for him, his scream had woken Mittens up.

Mittens poked his head out of the stroller to see what was going on. He noticed a little mouse sneaking into the restaurant. He leaped out of the stroller and jumped from table to table chasing after it. Everyone in the restaurant watched in horror. Mittens continued chasing the mouse until he saw it crawling on the waiter's shoe. He had to get it.

Bella and Rosie noticed what he was about to do, and in unison they called out, "No, Mittens! Not the waiter."

But it was too late. Mittens jumped onto the waiter. Startled, the waiter let go of a tray full of drinks in his hands and they crashed onto the floor. Gogo realised that things were getting out of control. She grabbed Mittens, and called the girls to follow her.

"My apologies," she said, heading for the door of the restaurant. "No more mischief from you," she whispered to Mittens.

As they set off in the car, Gogo told the girls that she was taking them to see Bella's cousin Tapiwa, who lived in the village. He managed to keep still. That is, until they came to an enormous misty waterfall, with a bright rainbow shining through it.

"It's so beautiful," smiled Bella.

"That's the Victoria falls," said Gogo, "I will take you there another time."

Meanwhile, Mittens was getting bored of being stuck in the car. He began to scratch restlessly at the car door, demanding to be let out.

Seeing this, Gogo stopped at a rest stop near a group of famous caves. As soon as the car door was opened, Mittens headed for the caves, eager to explore.

"No Mittens. Come back," shouted Rosie, running behind him.

Once in, they all chased Mittens through the dark caves, up the stairs and into a narrow passage. At the end of the passage bright light was shining through the caves. They came to a huge cavern opening up to the sky above and Bella could see the sunlight shimmering on the deep blue pool of water at the bottom. She glanced around the pool and there, at the water's edge, was Mittens. Rosie ran towards him and placed him into a cat carrier.

All of a sudden Gogo dived into the pool.

The girls were about to join her when they realised that Mittens could not jump into the pool with them and if they left him alone he would cause trouble again. As Rosie wondered what to do, she noticed a man wandering in the caves by the bushes.

"I will keep your fancy box safe," said the man, grinning and rubbing his hands together. The girls did not know that the man had readily agreed to hold the box because he thought there was something valuable inside. As soon as their backs were turned, he rushed off with the box and showed it to his friends.

They all huddled together, in a corner, not too far from the caves wondering what riches lay inside. But to their dismay, there was no treasure. Instead, Mittens popped his head out and stared up at them with his big green eyes.

"Miaow!" he purred.

The thieves shuddered.

"Aargh. Katsi!" yelled one of the men.

"We don't want bad luck," added the other. "Take it back."

The man closed the box and went to give it back to Rosie.

"Thank you, kind man," she said, walking back to Gogo's car, quite unaware of Mitten's adventure.

Soon they reached the village where Bella's cousin Tapiwa lived. Tapiwa's family lived on a farm. Their home was surrounded by mango trees and small farm-yard animals.

As they arrived, Tapiwa ran to the car to greet them, "Gogo!" she shouted. "Let me help you with your bags," she offered, not noticing Mittens who was ready to jump out of the car.

Tapiwa saw the cat and let out a loud scream. Although she looked after many animals, Tapiwa had not looked after a cat before. She had heard only bad stories about them. This frightened her so she was wary of Mittens.

Luckily, Bella convinced Tapiwa to give Mittens a chance, hoping he would behave himself. However, no sooner had they arrived than Mittens started to cause havoc.

He had been sleeping in the car for a long time and he now had a sudden burst of energy. Within seconds, he jumped from Rosie's arms and raced into the kitchen. There, he ran around knocking over everything in his path. He bumped into three big black pots that were stacked on top of each other. The pots wobbled from side to side, spilling water all over the cleanly swept floor until they finally fell down.

Tapiwa rushed after Mittens, mopping the mess he had made but nothing could stop him. Bella and Rosie ran behind Tapiwa telling her that Mittens meant no harm. It had all become one big circus!

That evening, Gogo and Tapiwa taught the girls how to cook traditional Zimbabwean food; sadza and peanut butter stew. Once dinner was ready, Rosie went to call Mittens. When she got to the room, something was very wrong.

Panicking, Rosie shouted, "Bella! Mittens is not in his box."

She searched high and low for him but he was nowhere to be found. Bella tried to keep calm and think of where Mittens could possibly be. But, she too, could not find him anywhere.

Meanwhile, out of the corner of her eye, Tapiwa caught sight of Mittens, who was climbing up one of the mango trees in the yard.

"Maybe he's better off up there," she thought to herself, remembering the mess he had made. Bella and Rosie continued to hunt for him.

"Mittens," yelled Bella. "Mittens, come back."

"Where is he?" wailed Rosie.

Tapiwa felt bad. She did not want anyone to feel sad. So she called to them.

"He's up there," she said, pointing up at the tree. Rosie called his name over and over again but Mittens would not come down. She tried to tempt him with his favourite treats but he did not move.

"How are we going to get him down?" asked Rosie.

"Let's call the fire brigade," suggested Bella.

"The fire brigade won't come to the village to rescue a cat stuck in a tree," laughed Tapiwa. "Don't worry. I'll go and get her."

Cautiously, Tapiwa climbed up the mango tree. With each step she climbed, Mittens moved further and further away as he was scared to come down. When she looked into his green eyes she could see how scared he was. The closer she moved towards him the more he purred. His purrs sounded like the cries of a baby. It was then that Tapiwa finally understood. Mittens did not mean to cause any trouble.

"It's okay," said Tapiwa in a calm voice. "I will keep you safe."

At once, he jumped into her arms and she slowly brought him back down.

Bella and Rosie were so happy that Tapiwa had helped to bring Mittens to safety, they rushed to hug them both. Bella was very proud of her cousin.

"Well done, Tapiwa!" smiled Bella. Tapiwa was no longer scared of Mittens, and she wanted to spend time with him even though he still caused trouble from time to time.

It had been a fun day. Bella could not believe she had ever been bored. She could not wait to explore more of Zimbabwe with Gogo, Tapiwa, Rosie and Mittens.

The Witch Doctor

Ethiopia

Since Bella and her parents had arrived in Ethiopia, they had allowed her to join them while they worked. She tagged along as they studied the magnificent Gondar castles built for Ethiopian kings and she even had the chance to climb the Simien mountains where Bella was thrilled to see many wild animals, some of which Dad told her are rare and only found in Ethiopia.

However, this week Bella could not join her parents. They were busy working in another town, examining royal tombs of ancient Ethiopian empresses. Instead she had to stay with her parents' friends, the Dibabas. Hakim and Halima, their twins, were known for pulling pranks. They loved playing pranks on everyone but Bella was fed up of it. She had even tried to get back at them but it was no use. Hakim and Halima knew all the tricks; no prank could ever fool them.

The twins father, Mr Dibaba, owned a tuck shop. Every now and again the twins would help out at his tuck shop while he was away but they couldn't resist pulling pranks. Today was no different. Mr Dibaba had left the twins in charge of the shop. They began to teach Bella how to run the shop and serve customers. After a while, Bella's first customer, an elderly man, approached the tuck shop.

He looked inside and asked for a bag of coffee and a dozen eggs. Bella glanced around the tuck shop searching for the items, when she saw Hakim and Halima stood in a corner with their hands over their mouth, giggling. As she reached to pick up a bag of coffee beans, Halima let out a loud laugh. Bella looked at her puzzled. The moment Bella picked up the bag, a great load of beans spilled across the floor. She had no idea that the bottom of the bag had been cut open.

"Look at what you've done," shouted Bella, "now he will have to buy his coffee elsewhere."

Bella picked up a box of eggs for the customer and continued serving. However, Halima was still laughing from the incident. In fact, she was laughing so hard, she tripped over the coffee beans and bumped into Bella as she fell. The box of eggs fell from Bella's hands and dropped, splattering all over the customer's shoes, just as she was handing them to him.

"Oh no," cried Bella, rushing over to get a cloth for the customer to clean his shoes.

The twins apologised to the customer and were about to run away when Mr Dibaba walked into the shop.

"Oh dear," said Mr Dibaba, staring at the coffee beans all over his shop floor. Before anyone could speak Mr Dibaba already knew exactly who was responsible.

"It was his idea!" said Halima, pointing to Hakim.

"No, she was the one who thought of it first," Hakim argued.

Mr Dibaba had heard it all before too many times. "No arguments," he said, sternly, "I don't want you to play anymore of your childish pranks. You have caused enough trouble."

As the twins helped to clear the shop, Bella decided to get away from them. She went into the house, where Mrs Dibaba was preparing food. "At least nothing can go wrong in here," she thought.

"What are you making Mrs Dibaba?" asked Bella.

"I'm making a pastry called sambusa. They are like samosas," smiled Mrs Dibaba, handing her an apron. "You can join me if you like."

Bella dipped her hands into the bowl and grabbed a ball of pastry. Before long they were kneading the dough together. Mrs Dibaba showed her how to fill the samosas and carefully shape them into little triangles. Bella was finally having fun when they heard the baby wailing.

"Please tidy up," said Mrs Dibaba, as she dashed out to comfort the baby.

Bella had almost finished tidying up when Hakim and Halima suddenly burst into the kitchen.

They stood at opposite ends of the kitchen, shoved a handful of food into their pockets and then stared at each other not saying a word. Bella knew exactly what was about to happen.

"Don't even think about it!" she warned.

But within seconds one of them yelled, "Food fight!" and the air was filled with flying food. Then, Hakim threw a pie at Halima. But she quickly ducked and it splattered all over Bella's clothes.

"This is the last straw," thought Bella.

She grabbed a handful of raisins and aimed them at Hakim. They all continued to hurl food across the room, laughing all the while, unaware that Mrs Dibaba was on her way back. As soon as she entered the kitchen she gasped. She could not believe what she was seeing.

"Stop!" yelled Mrs Dibaba, looking at the state of the kitchen.

Everyone stood in silence.

"I want you all to clean the kitchen this instance," she commanded, "I have special guests visiting and I don't want you to play any more pranks."

As they were cleaning the kitchen, Mrs Dibaba fried her sambusas in a large pan until they were golden brown. Then, she placed them on the window sill to cool down. The irresistible smell of the sambusas filled the air. Hakim's tummy rumbled. His mother was an excellent cook and always prepared the most delicious meals.

"Mmm," said Halima with a smile on her face. "Are you thinking what I'm thinking?" she whispered to Hakim.

The twins left the room and agreed to play one last prank. Sneakily, they poked their heads around the door and tiptoed into the kitchen. Their mother was nowhere to be seen and so Halima quickly snatched the plate full of the sambusas. Quietly, they crept down the hallway, step by step, until they were finally in their bedroom.

Bella was in her room when she saw them walk past. Curiously she followed them and peered into their room.

"What are you two up to now?" she asked.

"We are about to eat these sambusas," answered Halima, bursting with excitement.

"But won't your mother wonder where they are?" asked Bella.

"That's the best bit," replied Halima. "We are going to replace her sambusas with wet soggy bread.

We will decorate it just like the sambusas but when she takes a bite she will be in for a surprise," laughed Hakim. "It will be hilarious!"

"Why don't you join us," said Halima. "You never have any fun with us."

Bella had tried not to join in with their pranks but this had made her feel left out. She wanted to have fun too.

"What's the worst that could happen anyway?" she thought.

So Bella decided to join in with their prank.

"But first let's eat," said Halima, through a mouthful of food.

Bella grabbed a sambusa and stuffed it in her mouth. It was the most delicious pastry she had ever tasted. Hakim took a big bite, then another, and another! He licked his fingers and carried on leaving a trail of crumbs on the floor. They ate and ate until they could eat no more.

"Oh, I think I ate too much," said Halima, as she laid on her bed clutching her full stomach.

It was at that moment that they looked at the plate and realised there was nothing left. They finished working on their prank, and placed the fake food into the kitchen. Soon after, Mrs Dibaba's guests came through the door. As they sat, Mrs Dibaba brought the sambusas over. Hakim, Halima and Bella peaked through a small crack in the door and watched as the guests spat out the food.

Within a few moments, a voice called out, "Hakim, Halima, Bella! Come here this instant!"

They all hurried back to the kitchen and there, standing by the window sill, was Mrs Dibaba. "Someone ate the sambusas I had prepared for my guests and replaced it with this soggy bread," she said sternly. "Do any of you know who did this?"

Nervously, they all looked at each other and shrugged their shoulders. The twins had never seen their mother looking so cross before. In fact, Mrs Dibaba was so cross she decided to do something she had never done before.

"If no one knows what happened to my pastry then I have no choice," said Mrs Dibaba, "I will have to call a witch doctor."

A while later, she came back and announced that a witch doctor would be coming the next day. Scared, the twins ran out of the house and scrambled under a tree. They did not know what to do. Their mother had never called the witch doctor before. Bella, on the other hand, was confused about what had just happened.

"What's a witch doctor?" she asked.

"A witch doctor is a witch who has powers," explained Hakim. "They can heal the sick, see the past and the future."

"But they can also curse you or make bad things happen," added Halima.

This made Bella worry.

"I don't want anything bad to happen to me," she cried.

"You have to promise you won't say anything," pleaded Hakim, "or we will all be in big trouble."

That night, Bella was hungry but she hardly ate her dinner. When Mum and Dad arrived back from work their stories about the powerful Ethiopian empresses did not interest her. She curled up in bed with her stuffed elephant, tossing and turning, thinking about the witch doctor.

"Could they really see the past? What would they do if they found out that we ate the sambusas?" she wondered.

The next day, Bella and the twins sat and anxiously waited for the witch doctor.

Not long after they heard loud footsteps coming from inside the house. Together, they whipped round and looked behind them. The front door of their house swung open and a tall man appeared. He was at least six feet tall, with big bug eyes and a white zigzag mark across his face. Gasping, they held each other's hands tightly.

"Come inside," he said, "we must start."

Bella stood still, unsure of what to do.

"Should I tell the truth now?" she thought.

The witch doctor gathered everyone around and sat them down in a circle. There was a silence. Slowly, he unzipped his velvet bag and reached inside, wriggling his left hand back and forth. Bella squinted at it, trying to see what was inside the bag. He took out what looked like a bunch of leaves, red powder and potions. Then he laid them on the table next to a pot.

He started to mix the potions in different bottles humming a low chant, "Hu ma ma, Hu ma ma, Hu ma ma."

He poured them into a pot and he threw in a bunch of leaves, stirring the potions

together. After a while, the pot began to bubble.

"Hu ma ma, Hu ma ma, Hu ma ma," the witch doctor continued, as he poured everything from his bag into the pot.

All of a sudden, a cloud of red smoke escaped from the pot. Without warning, the witch doctor began to grow taller. His nails grew longer and longer until they did not look like nails at all. They were long and bony, like the twigs of a tree. Then he began to cackle to himself, pouring the lumpy potion from the big black pot into three small cups.

"Put out your hands!" he commanded, handing a small blue cup to each of them.

"I'd rather not!" blurted Hakim. Reluctantly, they held onto the cups and a terrible odour flew into their noses.

"Once you drink the potion, whoever ate the sambusas will suddenly feel their belly slowly getting bigger and bigger and bigger," he warned.

The twins glanced at each other, then at Bella. At once they all shouted, "It was us! It was us!"

"I should have told the truth," cried Bella.

"Don't worry," said the witch doctor. "I would never harm you."

"Your parents sent me here to play a prank on you," he confessed to Hakim and Halima.

At that point Mr and Mrs Dibaba walked into the room along with Bella's parents. "It's okay to play a few harmless jokes once in a while but when you do it all the time it becomes intolerable," said Mrs Dibaba.

The twins were surprised that their parents had played a trick on them all along. Mrs Dibaba told them they had to do chores for the rest of the week as punishment.

Then, the witch doctor collected his potions and was ready to leave. But, it was now dark and chilly outside. So, Mrs Dibaba invited him for dinner. She had cooked injera with lentil stew. The witch doctor could not resist Mrs Dibaba's food so he stayed. Dad loved it so much he got a second helping. After dinner, the witch doctor sat everyone around the warm campfire and he told spooky stories until it was time for him to go.

As Bella warmed her hands by the fire, she did not feel so unlucky for staying with the twins anymore. She also realised that she did not have to pull pranks with them to fit in. As for Hakim and Halima, they still loved playing pranks but they only ever did so once in a while. After all, who knows what trick their parents might pull on them next.

Finding Cuddles

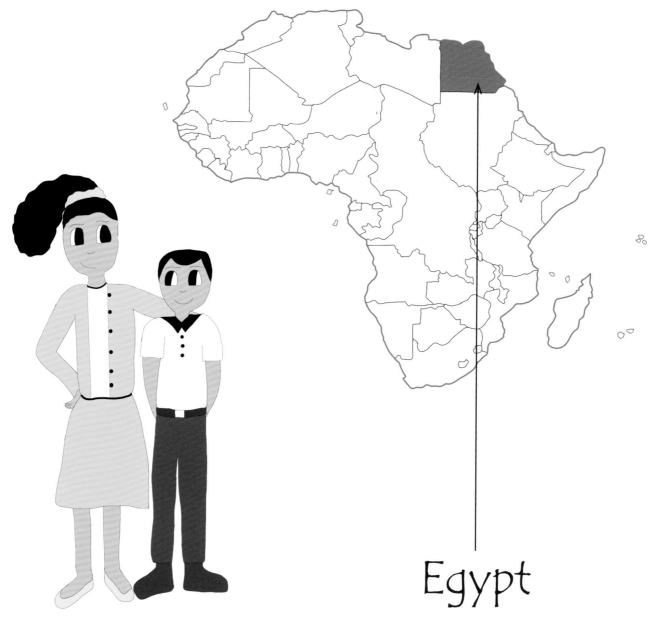

Egypt

Bella's favourite stuffed toy elephant, Cuddles, was missing. It had been only two days since they had arrived in Egypt and already she had lost something. Her grandmother, Gogo, had sewn Cuddles for her when she was little and every night ever since, Cuddles had slept beside her. So now that Cuddles was missing, how could Bella possibly get to sleep?

That night she quietly tiptoed out of her room, careful not to make a sound, and went to search for Cuddles.

In the darkness she cautiously felt her way along the hallway until she reached the kitchen. It was the only place left in the house that she had not searched. She reached into a cupboard that stood high above her head, and accidentally knocked over one of the pans, which then fell onto her head, covering her eyes.

"Ouch!" she yelled.

At that very moment someone entered the kitchen.

"What's all the noise about?" said the person who was now behind her.

Looking back over her shoulder, Bella saw Lala, who was holding onto a small lantern. Bella was ashamed to tell her about Cuddles but she needed her help.

Lala was full of ideas and always knew what to do, even though she was a bit bossy at times. So Bella told her all about Cuddles.

"Have you asked your parents if they know where Cuddles is?" she asked.

"No, I promised them that I would look after my belongings well. I don't want them to think I can't look after my things properly," she sighed.

"Don't worry Bella," said Lala. "I will help you to find it."

They searched drawer after drawer, cupboard after cupboard but there was no sign of Cuddles. As Lala knelt down to look into the cupboards again, she had an idea. If they went back to all the places they had visited the day before then surely they would find Cuddles. Feeling hopeful, Lala shared her idea with Bella. But just then, the sound of footsteps on creaking floorboards startled them.

"Shh!" whispered Bella, "someone's coming."

The girls crouched under the table when all of a sudden they heard, "boo!"

They looked up and saw a little boy with the biggest grin on his face, laughing.

"Yusuf. You are the most annoying little brother in the world!" said Lala angrily.

"No I'm not," he frowned, grabbing at Lala's lantern.

"Oh no, you don't! That lantern is mine!" she said, trying to pull it out of Yusuf's hands.

As they pulled it back and forth, on opposite ends, the lantern slipped out of their hands and smashed loudly onto the floor, breaking into little pieces.

Mr Arafa, their father, was woken by the noise. He came running into the kitchen and commanded them to go back to bed. But Bella was optimistic.

"At least now we have a plan to find Cuddles," she thought.

That morning, everyone set off to go to the market but Bella and Lala pleaded to go to the pyramids instead, as Lala thought they might have left him there during their trip the previous day.

"The pyramids? Why do they want to go there again?" wondered Yusuf.

When they arrived at the pyramids, Bella and Lala quickly climbed onto the back of a camel, eager to search for the stuffed elephant.

"Wait for me!" yelled Yusuf, who was struggling to get on his camel.

The girls were so preoccupied with searching for Cuddles that they did not hear Yusuf calling. They had been riding for ages when Lala caught sight of something familiar in the distance.

"The museum," she said. "We went to the museum yesterday!"

In a hurry, the girls jumped off the camel and hatched a plan. Yusuf looked at them, puzzled.

"What are they up to now?" he wondered, "and why do they want to go to the museum again?"

Fortunately for the girls, Mr Arafa worked at the museum and he was happy for them to join him. So he offered to take them inside while Bella's parents went to the Valley of the Kings to examine the tombs of Egyptian Pharaohs.

As they entered the museum, the girls were ready to begin searching for Cuddles but Mr Arafa interrupted them.

"There's a competition at the museum today," he said. "Whoever can create the best sphinx wins a special prize."

"A prize," shouted Yusuf excitedly. "A special prize! We've got to win it."

"But we wanted to do something else," protested Lala.

"No arguments. I want you all to work together and create something special!" said Mr Arafa, walking away. The girls had no choice but to do as they were told.

Excited to get on with the task, Yusuf began, "Before we get started, I will explain what a sphinx is. A sphinx guards the pyramids. It has the head of a pharaoh and the body of a lion."

But Lala interrupted him. "We know what a sphinx is. Let's just get started," she said, keen to finish the task quickly.

Yusuf ran around collecting all the materials they needed. Before long they were having so much fun working together to create the sphinx that they forgot about Cuddles. They were almost finished when Yusuf went off to get some paint to decorate their Sphinx.

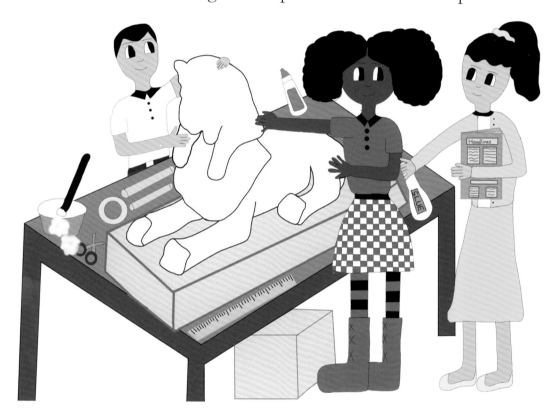

The girls continued working on the Sphinx when Bella suddenly caught a glimpse of the clock. It was already midday.

"If we work as quickly as possible, we will still have time to look for your toy," said Lala. "After all, that was the reason we came here in the first place."

But what Bella and Lala had not realised was that Yusuf, who had been standing in the doorway, had overheard their conversation.

Yusuf finally understood why the girls had been acting strange all day. He watched as Bella grabbed the head of the sphinx, smeared glue all over it and sloppily stuck it onto the body. But the head was still wobbly. Yusuf ran back into the room, and caught the head before it fell off.

He was annoyed that the girls were ruining his perfect creation just so they could hurry and find Bella's toy but he tried to not let it bother him and carefully painted the head with gold and blue paint. As he turned to look at the body, he noticed that the girls were already painting it pink with blue spots.

"Oh no. You are using the wrong colours to paint it," he gasped. "It's not supposed to look like that at all!"

"Go away Yusuf," snapped Lala, shoving him aside, "you are spoiling our fun!"

Yusuf stormed out of the room. "I was only trying to make the best sphinx," he yelled.

"Aw, poor Yusuf," said Bella sadly.

She hurried after him but it was too late. He was gone. She knew she should have listened to him but she wanted to find Cuddles.

"Quick! Let's look now before he comes back," said Lala.

"We were in that room yesterday," pointed Bella, "let's search in there."

Inside the room there were statues and drawings on the walls. A polished golden tomb was set in the middle. It had belonged to a famous pharaoh in ancient Egypt called King Tutankhamun. His great treasures filled the room. Searching the room, Bella was startled by a strange noise by the window.

"What was that?" she asked, looking around. "It's just the wind," replied Lala.

She had been to that room a thousand times and she knew that there was nothing to fear. However, Bella was not so sure. Slowly, she walked towards the sound, listening closely. Her heart was racing.

"Aargh," she yelled, as she heard an echo from the tomb.

"It's probably nothing," said Lala, trying to remain calm.

But then the echoing grew louder and louder.

Terrified, they charged out of the room and ran into the next one, determined to find Cuddles.

The room was filled with priceless treasures but there was something about it that frightened them. Then Bella felt a cold chill in the air and the door slammed hard behind them.

At once, they leapt up onto a tomb, knocking over a precious vase. The vase clattered loudly onto the floor. As Bella looked down, she saw something odd.

There, hidden behind a tomb, was a hand wrapped in white tissue waving at them. This time both girls screamed as loud as they could. Their voices echoed through the corridors of the museum. They screamed so loud that the figure came out from behind the tomb laughing.

"It's only me," said Yusuf, taking the bandages from his face.

He had disguised himself as a mummy. But it was too late. Lala could not stop screaming and a crowd had gathered. Peering through her fingers, Bella realised that all the visitors at the museum were now standing in front of them, gasping at all the commotion. To make matters worse, Mr Arafa was stood in front of them, shaking his head. His face was as red as a tomato and he looked as if he was ready to pop.

"Yusuf, why are you scaring the girls? he scolded. "These statues are a very important part of our history. I don't want anything to happen to them!"

"But the girls weren't taking the competition seriously," replied Yusuf.

"It's not the winning that matters. It's about taking part and working well together!" said Mr Arafa.

At that moment, they all realised that they should not have behaved the way they had. The girls apologised to Mr Arafa and Yusuf.

Bella explained to Mr Arafa that she had lost her stuffed elephant and that she and Lala could think of nothing but finding it. It was then that Mr Arafa told her that he had found a stuffed toy elephant in the museum the previous day but he had no idea that it belonged to Bella.

"It must have fell out of my bag," said Bella.

Bella felt silly. She had gone through so much trouble when all she had to do was be ask Mr Arafa.

"It's nothing to be ashamed of," he smiled. "I still cling onto a special blanket that my mother gave to me when I was young. It means a lot to me."

Just then a deep voice was heard in the room, "Ahem. Silence please. It's time for us to reveal the winner of the competition."

Hearing this, Yusuf remembered that their sphinx was very different from the ones everyone else had made.

"There's no point staying to hear the winner," he thought, "there is no way we could have possibly won."

Just as he turned to walk away, he heard the voice continuing, "And the winners are Bella, Yusuf and Lala! Your sphinx was unique. We were all very impressed."

Proudly, they held up their trophy, as everyone cheered and applauded. They could not believe they had won. They jumped up and punched the air.

"Woo hoo!" screamed Bella.

The Treasure Hunt

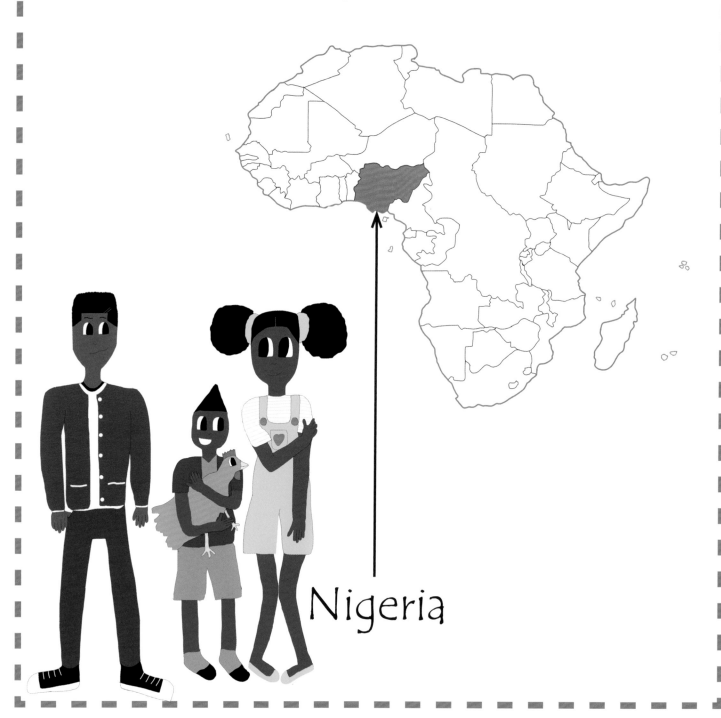

Nigeria

It was the day before Aunt Fumi's wedding. Aunt Fumi was Mum's little sister. Mum had grown up in Nigeria and she had always told Bella so many stories about her family. Bella could not wait to finally meet all her other relatives. But her cousin Temi, did not share the same excitement.

She hated meeting new people. To make matters worse, her mother had invited far too many people and every time someone entered the living room she never quite knew what to say.

Luckily, her best friend Chinedu had also been invited. Confident Chinedu. He always knew the right thing to say and he was friendly.

"Auntie!" he shouted as he walked into the room. "I am so happy to see you."

Right behind him was Bella's cousin, Yoma, who liked to tease Temi.

"Shall we go somewhere else for a while?" suggested Bella who had noticed that Temi was still feeling anxious.

Temi nodded. They were about to leave when Temi's mother spotted them.

"Temi, you must take your brother Tobi with you," she said, pointing to the little boy who was behind her, chasing his pet hen.

"But mum, he always brings that hen with him!" groaned Temi.

Just then, Temi caught sight of Yoma's friends, who were sniggering, as they watched Tobi chasing his hen. "Who keeps a hen as a pet?" one of them sneered.

Temi felt embarrassed. Bella turned to her and fiercely asked, "What is so wrong with having a hen for a pet?"

They had nothing to say and so Bella, Temi and Chinedu ran into the hallway, chasing after Tobi and his hen. There, at the other end of the hallway, with the bird safely in his arms, was Tobi.

"You really should take better care of that hen," said Temi.

But Tobi was not paying attention. He was staring at a small green wooden door that was underneath the staircase. It had an unusual handle and there was a sign taped to the door which read, "Keep out."

Bella wondered why the door was so small. "What could possibly be inside?" she wondered.

KEEP
OUT!

"I'm not sure we should go there Bella," said Temi, who was afraid of exploring somewhere new.

But Bella was already kneeling down and turning the strange door handle.

"It's okay Temi. Let's just have a peek then we'll go back," reassured Chinedu.

As Bella opened the door it revealed a flight of stairs that led down to the basement. Bella held onto the creaky banister, feeling her way down the stairs with everyone else behind her. The floor was covered in sticky grime but still they carried on walking until they reached another door, which opened into an abandoned room.

Inside were boxes sealed with black tape, and an old painting swung crookedly making a squeaking sound. Dusty Cobwebs hung from every corner of the room and old newspapers were scattered everywhere. As they were looking around the room, Yoma and her friends quietly entered it. They hid behind the door but one of them stumbled. The noise startled Temi.

"Bella, I think we should go back," she whispered.

They were about to leave the room when Tobi suddenly shouted, "My hen! Where's my hen?"

"Let's help him look for her," said Bella.

They searched for the hen everywhere. As Bella looked behind a barrel, she found a little golden box. Bella opened the box and inside was an ancient scroll. She unravelled the scroll, revealing a map. They all gathered around her and examined it.

Just then, Temi remembered a story her mother had told her about the lost treasure of an ancient Nigerian king and said, "There is a legend that a great king once lived in this town and had lots of treasure. Before he died, he hid his treasure somewhere in this house. However, lots of people have searched this house but no-one has ever found it."

"Treasure!" shouted Bella and Chinedu. "We should look for it too!"

Hearing their exclamations, Yoma and her friends could hardly contain their excitement.

Bella, Chinedu, Tobi and Temi started searching the room, inch by inch, but the treasure was nowhere to be found.

Bella examined the map again but they could not understand what the symbols on the map represented. "If only we could find out how to read the map," said Bella.

"If you come to my house we can use my mother's laptop to research more about the treasure on the internet," suggested Chinedu.

When they arrived at Chinedu's house they did not have much time to research. His mother had already cooked dinner and insisted they stayed for it. She brought out large plates of pounded yum and egusi soup. "Can I have a knife and fork?" asked Bella, sitting down next to Temi. "You can use a knife and fork for rice but we eat pounded yam with our hands," smiled Temi.

As they ate, Bella wondered how the treasure could possibly be in Aunt Fumi's house when they had searched every inch of the basement. But they were all too exhausted to think about it anymore. After the meal, they sat and watched a Nollywood film before Temi's mother took them home.

Meanwhile, Yoma and her friends were still in the basement searching for the treasure. "We've got to find the treasure first," said Yoma.

Yoma and her friends searched for hours, but they could not find the treasure.

Early the next morning, the girls were awoken by a tapping sound on their bedroom window. There, stood in front of the window was Chinedu who was ready to go and have another look for the treasure before the wedding started.

"I managed to search the internet and I was able to work out what the symbols on the map represent," said Chinedu.

The girls quickly got dressed and ran to the garage to get some bikes. Temi hopped onto her bike and Chinedu shared his with Bella, while Tobi slowly cycled behind them in his tricycle. Before long, they reached Aunt Fumi's house.

However, it was the day of the wedding and there were a lot of people inside the house. Bella peeked inside, and could see Mum and the other ladies getting ready. How were they going to get past them?

Quietly they crept into the house, desperate not to catch their attention. Luckily for them, there was so much chaos inside the house. The bride had broken her shoe and she was in tears. Temi's mother and everyone else were too busy trying to keep the bride calm to see them crawling past. But when they reached the attic, they realised someone had already been there before them. The door was wide open and everything was scattered everywhere. Not a box had been left unturned.

"Let's use the map to see if the treasure is still here," said Bella.

But Hidden behind the boxes was Yoma and her friends, who had been watching them silently. They leaped up and headed for the map.

"Thank you for you for bringing back the map," laughed Yoma, as she tried to grab the map from Bella's hands.

But Bella held it above her head and refused to give it to them. Then Yoma had an idea. She ran and grabbed Tobi's hen instead.

Bella ran towards her but Yoma warned, "You better give me the map or we are keeping the hen." Bella stared at Tobi's teary eyes and knew what she had to do. "You can have the map but I want the hen back, safe and sound," she said.

Hesitantly, Bella handed Yoma the map. Then the hen flapped its wings and flew into Tobi's arms. Feeling smug, Yoma and her friends grabbed the map.

They tried their best but they could not figure out what the symbols on the map meant. "We are going to go and get the code for this map. Once we figure out what these symbols mean, the treasure will be ours," said Yoma, walking out of the room.

Frustrated, Bella, Temi and Chinedu sat disappointed. They were never going to find the treasure now.

"Let's just go and get ready for the wedding," said Temi.

They were about to leave when they heard Tobi crying, "My hen, I can't find her!"

"Not again!" said Temi.

They looked all over the room, but this time they could not find her. A while later, Bella heard a clucking sound coming from somewhere in the room. The closer she moved towards the bookshelf, the more she could hear the sound. As she moved one of the books from shelf, a trap door opened from underneath her legs. Bella fell through and landed into another room. Chinedu, Temi and Tobi followed behind. There, in a corner of the room, was the treasure chest. Their eyes grew wide in amazement. Inside were mountains of glistening gold and sparkling jewels.

"Woah!" gasped Bella. She could not believe her eyes.

"We are rich! We are rich!" exclaimed Temi, hugging Bella and Chinedu.

As for Tobi, he cuddled his hen which had been hiding behind the bookshelf. They quickly dragged the treasure back into the basement.

At that very moment, Mum burst into the room. "Bella, I've been looking for you everywhere. The wedding is about to start any minute now!"

They explained their adventure to Mum, who examined the treasure and recognised the coins. "This once belonged to an ancient king of the Kingdom of Benin. It is a very important part of Nigeria's history," she said with delight.

Immediately, she called the police, who came to collect the treasure and promised to take it to a museum. They even gave them five gold coins each as a reward. When Yoma and her friends came back, they were surprised to see that the treasure had already been found.

"Well done for finding the treasure," said Yoma to Temi.

Yoma and her friends apologised to them all and realised if they had all worked together they would have received a reward too. Soon after, they all left the basement and enjoyed Aunt Fumi's wedding. Everyone sang and danced all day and Bella enjoyed meeting all her relatives.

Bella's Birthday

Tanzania

As Bella stepped into the warm rainforest which was at the bottom of Mount Kilimanjaro in Tanzania, she was greeted by the most wonderful animals. Around her she could hear the soft sounds of the river flowing, insects fluttering and birds chirping in the trees. High up the tall trees she could see black and white monkeys jumping from tree to tree, jumping higher than she thought possible.

"This is exactly how I wanted to spend my birthday," she said to Mum.

Her parents had gone to great lengths to organise this for her, as Bella had specifically asked them to arrange this so she could see all the wonderful animals of the rainforest. They had even arranged for their next door neighbour Jamal and his sisters, Aaliyah and Khadijah, to come along. But, despite all this, she felt as though something was missing.

Secretly, she wished she could also celebrate her birthday with all the friends she had met during her journey across Africa, especially since she was flying back to England the next day. But she did not want to disappoint her parents, as she had asked them to arrange the trip to the rainforest. She continued down the trail and listened as Jamal told them all about the rainforest. He had read several books about it and had been there lots of times before.

"The Colobus monkeys are the only monkeys that have no thumbs," he said. He stopped when he noticed how sad Bella looked. "What's wrong?" he asked. When Bella told Jamal, he exclaimed, "I know just what to do!"

Bella glanced at Jamal, wondering what he was thinking.

"Let's have a party," he said excitedly. "My mother could bake you her delicious doughnut cakes and I can tell your parents it was my idea if you are worried about what they might say."

"We must get some chapatis," added Aaliyah, "you can't have a party without chapattis."

Finally, everything was working out well.

"It's nearly noon, let's hurry up and get started," said Jamal.

Bella called to Mum and Dad and they all rushed to the car. As they were driving back, Bella remembered that they had not invited anyone else.

"Oh no. This is a disaster!" she said. "Don't worry," said Mum with a warm smile.

"I'm sure everything will be just fine."

As they arrived back at the house they were staying, Bella swung the door open. A moment later, her eyes lit up and a big grin spread across her face. "SUPRISE!" yelled everyone in the room.

"We knew you secretly wanted to celebrate with your friends so we planned a surprise for you," said Mum tenderly, and gave her a kiss on her forehead.

Bella could not have been happier.

Inside, there was a big sign with, "Happy birthday!" written on it, balloons at every corner of the room and presents stacked up against the wall.

Her best friend Rosie flung her arms around her and smiled, "I wasn't going to miss your birthday for anything."

Before she could respond, her grandmother, Gogo, who had travelled all the way from Zimbabwe came to squeeze her cheeks. "My little girl is all grown up!" she said proudly.

As Bella glanced down at herself, she realised she was still wearing muddy boots and was definitely not dressed for a party. She dashed upstairs and quickly got dressed. As she came down, she saw Thandiwe and Johan standing at the bottom of the stairs, holding a huge present wrapped in a big white bow. Next to them stood a girl and her little brother who was carrying a neatly wrapped present.

"What did you get her?" Johan asked the little boy.

"I got her a small statue of a sphinx," whispered Yusuf to Johan.

This annoyed his sister Lala. "We both got it for her!" she snapped.

But before she could continue, she was interrupted by a knock at the door.

At the door, dressed in his finest clothes, was Pierre from Côte d'Ivoire. "You look like a true African princess," he said smiling.

Just then, Mum and Dad entered the room carrying a huge chocolate cake. "Three, two, one! Happy birthday to you," they sang and soon everyone joined in.

It was turning out to be a lovely birthday.

However, in one corner, Hakim and Halima were giggling as they filled balloons with water preparing for a water balloon fight. In another corner, Mittens was busy knocking the drinks all over the floor and Rosie was running after him, trying to stop the chaos. Seeing this, Bella began to chase after Mittens too, but within a few seconds she bumped into Yusuf and Lala, who were tugging one of the presents, quarrelling about who would be the one to give it to Bella.

Then in the middle of the room, an argument erupted between Chinedu and Abena, about who had brought the tastiest jollof rice.

"Everyone knows that Nigerians cook the best jollof rice," said Chinedu.

This upset Abena. "No, no!" she said, stamping her foot crossly, "Ghanaian people cook it the best!"

Pierre had been listening to the conversation. He remembered the tasty jollof his mother always made for him so he added, "Actually the best jollof rice is made in Côte d'Ivoire."

Chinedu and Abena turned and stared at Pierre. Everyone else just watched the commotion. Bella tried to end the argument but nothing she said seemed to help.

"This is a disaster," she sighed, "everything was going wrong."

"Oh no," exclaimed Jamal, turning to Bella. "What are we going to do?"

Bella knew there was only one person who could save her party now.

She went out of the room and came back with Gogo. Gogo marched into the room and stood on a chair.

Firmly she yelled, "Quiet, everybody! I want you all to come here and sit in a circle."

Everyone turned their attention to Gogo and went to sit down.

"I'm going to tell you a story," announced Gogo, "and I want you all to listen very carefully. Long ago, there was an old lady who lived in a small village. One day she decided to cook a large meal for everyone in her village but she only had a few ingredients and just one pot. So, she decided to cook everything in one big pot using all the ingredients she had. She poured the rice into the pot, then tomatoes, onions, scotch bonnet peppers and a pinch of salt. A delicious aroma steamed from the pot as she stirred and stirred. When everyone tasted the rice, which was red in colour, they wanted more and more."

"The old lady became known for her special rice, which she named jollof. People came from all over the village just for a taste of the rice. One day she decided to leave the village and go on a journey across West Africa, just to share her recipe. She travelled up mountains and forests, crossing many valleys and rivers," explained Gogo.

"What happened next Gogo?" asked Bella curiously.

"She passed through Sierra Leone. They loved the jollof rice and decided to add to cabbage to their recipe to make it unique. Then she travelled to Ghana, where they added black pepper and served with chicken. In Nigeria they included ginger and served it with salad, plantains and moi moi. In Cameroon they added coconut milk. As she travelled through each country everyone added their own special ingredients. The old lady's recipe is now enjoyed by people from many nations. This happened so long ago that people have forgotten all about the old lady's story and her wish that everyone would make jollof rice in their own special way and for the jollof to bring people together," said Gogo.

Gogo looked at Chinedu and Abena and said, "It is only a child who has never travelled who says that only his mother prepares tasty meals."

Chinedu and Abena looked at each other and realised how silly they had been.

"I'm sorry Abena," said Chinedu, "I'm not used to trying new food."

"Me too," said Abena, "we should go and taste each other's jollof rice."

They both smiled and went to eat jollof together.

"Now all we need is some music," added Khadijah, "maybe Jamal can play his Ilimbla instrument."

Jamal pulled out a silver metal item with a row of keys from his bag and gently plucked the instrument with his fingers, playing lovely tune.

"I hope you like it," he said shyly.

"It's perfect!" exclaimed Bella.

They all clapped, cheered and danced as they listened to Jamal playing his ilimba.

Bella was very happy to see her friends finally getting along. For the rest of the day they enjoyed party activities, ate jollof and learnt about each other's culture. It was the best birthday she had ever had!